Dear Readers!

I felt something was missing at this particular time of the year, so with the help of my daughter, we came up with this two dad holiday book. Hope you all enjoy it and happy holidays!

-Jayke (and Makenna)

Dad and Daddy put me to bed,
Wearing my pajamas of all red,
And said go to sleep for
Christmas is ahead!

They both tuck me into
bed tight,
And say "I love you
kiddo, goodnight,"
As they walk out the room,
they turn out the light!

As I lay down I close my eyes,
Happy for my Christmas day
surprise,
And all the wonderful delicious
pies!

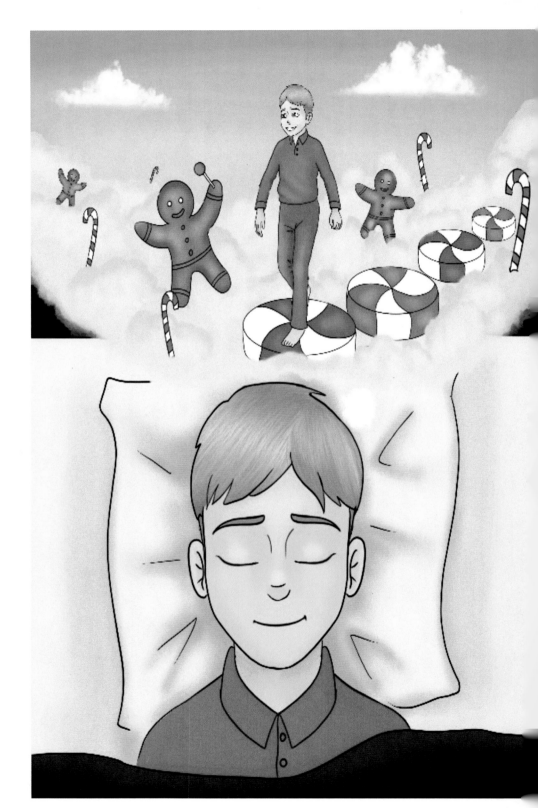

I fall into a deep, deep sleep,
Where the gingerbread people
all leap,
And I walk through a candy
cane path knee deep!

My the dream keeps going on
strong,
Walking through all the snow, I
belong,
But then hearing a familiar
Christmas song!

The song wakes me up and
I hear,
Talking from downstairs but
words unclear,
So I slowly go down the stairs
with some fear!

I gasp! Santa and daddy hear,
And go back to bed, to disappear,
Not sure if what I saw is as it appears!

Daddy kissed Santa on the lips.
My heart is racing and a beat skips,
But under the tree I saw one or two ships?

No matter, daddy kissed
St. Nick!
What does this mean, let me
think real quick,
Or was this my eyes playing
on me a trick?

I saw right. Does daddy love him?
Or was the kiss done on just a whim?
Does Santa have being a step-dad in him?

Santa as a step-dad...could he?
And I'd be Santa's stepson, yeah me!
I think that'd be cool, wouldn't you all agree?

What about my dad, where is he?
Having three dads would be cool for me!
Daily would feel like Christmas, with all the glee!

I will sleep knowing what I do.
Tomorrow I will tell my dads
who,
I saw daddy kiss on the steps;
in plain view!

I will awake for Christmas day
And see all my toys or just will
play,
For Christmas is here and mine
will for sure slay!

I want to see who's up this late,
Or could this be Santa Claus,
the great?
I walk step by step down as I
cannot wait!

I reach the bottom step and
peer…
Around the corner as I am near,
And now I listen and I clearly
do hear!

My daddy's saying "You look good,
Do not forget to pull down the hood
And even with that belly kiss me you should!"

I see a man in white and red
Lean down to my dad and tilt
his head,
And kisses daddy on the lips as
he said!

I will go to sleep good and
tight
And await the glow of morning
light.
Goodnight and dream of the
cold snow that is white!